THE MONTESSORI SYSTEM EXAMINED

MAXWELL PRESS

THE MONTESSORI SYSTEM EXAMINED

WILLIAM HEARD KILPATRICK

Associate Professor of the Philosophy of

Education Teachers College, Columbia University

MAXWELL PRESS

Chennai   New Delhi

MAXWELL PRESS

An Imprint of MJP Publishers

ISBN 978-93-5528-204-0   MAXWELL PRESS

All rights reserved
Printed and bound in India

No. 44, Nallathambi Street,
Triplicane,
Chennai 600 005

MJP 1414   © Publishers, 2022

Publisher :   **C. Janarthanan**

PUBLISHER'S NOTE

The legacy of a country is in its varied cultural heritage, historical literature, developments in the field of economy and science. The top nations in the world are competing in the field of science, economy and literature. This vast legacy has to be conserved and documented so that it can be bestowed to the future generation. The knowledge of this legacy is slowly getting perished in the present generation due to lack of documentation.

Keeping this in mind, the concern with retrospective acquiring of rare books has been accented recently by the burgeoning reprint industry. MAXWELL PRESS is gratified to retrieve the rare collections with a view to bring back those books that were landmarks in their time.

In this effort, a series of rare books would be republished under the banner, "MAXWELL PRESS". The books in the reprint series have been carefully selected for their contemporary usefulness as well as their historical importance within the intellectual. We reconstruct the book with slight enhancements made for better presentation, without affecting the contents of the original edition.

Most of the works selected for republishing covers a huge range of subjects, from history to anthropology. We believe this reprint edition will be a service to the numerous researchers and practitioners active in this fascinating field. We allow readers to experience the wonder of peering into a scholarly work of the highest order and seminal significance.

MAXWELL PRESS

PREFACE

The aim of this monograph is probably sufficiently indicated by the title. The purpose is to examine generally the educational doctrines promulgated by Dr. Maria Montessori, so as, first, to bring out their relation to one another and to other similar doctrines elsewhere held; and, second, to ascertain, as far as the author may, the contribution which Dr. Montessori has to offer to American education.

My indebtedness, especially in proportion to the volume of matter, is great. To my colleagues on an investigating trip to Rome, Miss Annie E. Moore and Professor M. B. Hillegas, I am indebted for very considerable assistance in the ordering of ideas and in reaching definite conclusions. My best thanks are due to the same two colleagues and to Professors John Dewey and Naomi Norsworthy for reading the manuscript and for making valuable suggestions. It would be unfair, however, to hold any one save the author responsible for the opinions herein expressed.

W. H. K.

CONTENTS

EDITOR'S INTRODUCTION

The labors of Madam Montessori have aroused an unusual interest among Americans. Already her theories and practices are a frequent subject for investigation and discussion in meetings of teachers and parents.

Among a considerable number of laymen and a smaller number of teachers, the interest amounts to enthusiasm. The doctrines of the Italian educator are so warmly espoused by some that schools modeled on the plan of the Casa dei Bambini have been established in various parts of the country, where they rival and challenge the existing kindergartens and primary schools. To many of its adherents this movement constitutes an educational revolution which in time will completely change the education of children.

The interest of the teaching profession as a whole is not marked by any such self-committal. The teachers are concerned to know the meaning of this agitation and are professionally curious to ascertain its worth for them. They are critical, if not skeptical; and they ask that the significance of this new expression of educational the-

EDITOR'S INTRODUCTION

ory be presented in terms of its practical bearing upon the teaching procedure commonly employed with young children. They are tolerant enough of new dogma and experiment; but they possess a common-sense caution against a too-ready acceptance of them. They prefer to examine a new program element by element, reserving the privilege of selecting and rejecting as their judgment decides. They would weigh every item of the idealistic projects of radicals and even of the practical successes of experiments born among the differing conditions of foreign soil. Willing enough to admit that any new movement may contain factors that will aid in educational evolution, they are not of the type completely to let go of one institution in order to seize another. They prefer the safer position of being reconstructors of the old.

While admitting the value of both types of thinkers and workers in the whole method of educational advance, it is to the relatively large group of public-school teachers and superintendents that this volume is addressed.

The smaller class of heroic enthusiasts that become the more or less partisan leaders and followers of a new propaganda are not likely to be interested in a critical analysis of the particular theories and practices that constitute their faith. With them the new institutional spirit is the thing! Details may be left to the rectification of time!

Not so with the leaders and teachers of the rank and file! To them the detail is the thing! Upon the soundness of special theories and the effectiveness of particular practices, the strength of an institutional scheme depends. They want to know how far the theory of Madam Montessori departs from the best philosophy of education that the American profession knows. And when it does, they ask if experience, of both scientific and empirical sort, gives warrant to the varying belief. More than this, they would ascertain if claims made for practical success are proved; and, again, if such achievements may be reproduced under the conditions of American life.

These pertinent inquiries of American teachers require a judicial answer. It is offered in the brief accompanying volume, along with such historical and logical perspective as is necessary to clear understanding.

THE MONTESSORI SYSTEM EXAMINED

I

INTRODUCTION

THE genesis of Madam Montessori's educational ideas is laid before the reader in simple but attractive manner in her principal work, *The Montessori Method*, as the English translation is called. But slight reference to the now well-known story is needed. Madam Montessori, as assistant physician at the Psychiatric Clinic of the University of Rome, became some fifteen years ago interested in defectives. She thus learned of the work done by Edward Seguin for the education of idiots. From this and from personal experimentation in the education of feeble-minded, there came the suggestion of using Seguin's method with the normal child. In this is found one important factor in the making of the Montessori method. While this study of defectives was going on, there had been organized in Milan a School of Scientific Pedagogy. The anthropologist Sergi appears to have been the leading spirit in the enterprise. The emphasis in this school was upon anthropometry and measurements in experimental psychology, particularly of the sensations. Whether from a more widespread interest or from the influence of this particular school does not certainly appear, but the field of scientific measurement constitutes another factor in the formation of the Montessori method. A third element was the general background of prevalent educational theory which one absorbs more or less unconsciously as one does his uncriticized religion or politics. This we may surmise was largely Pestalozzian in its ultimate origin. A fourth factor was the invitation extended to Madam Montessori by a building corporation in Rome to organize the infant schools in its model tenements. The effort to meet this demand created in large measure the Children's House, especially in its institutional aspect. In these four elements we seem to have the origin of the Montessori schools.

It is not necessary to the purpose at hand to show just how far Madam Montessori is indebted to Seguin for her didactic apparatus. No acknowledgment could be more open or generous than is hers; and every one acquainted with

INTRODUCTION

Seguin's work will be struck with the similarity.
There is, however, one important difference:
Seguin was interested mainly in leading the
defective to make those acquisitions of knowledge and skill which would with relative direct-
ness prove useful in the ordinary affairs of his
life; Madam Montessori, on the other hand, is
more interested — as we shall later discover —
in the disciplinary aspect of the exercises.

The study of science has had far-reaching effect
upon Madam Montessori and upon her educational theory. In the general wish to apply
scientific conceptions to education, few surpass
her. Those who feel the urgent need for a more
scientific study of education and for the bringing
of the scientific spirit into our attitude toward
educational practice, can but applaud the insistence with which Madam Montessori returns
again and again to this point of view. In addition
to the general demand for a scientific attitude on
the part of teachers, we find specific elements of
her procedure based on her scientific experience.
For example, the teacher must keep records, both
anthropometric and psychologic, of each child.
The books in which these are kept are often
shown to the visitor. The remark may be inter-
jected that the data so recorded, unfortunately,

hardly function otherwise than in keeping alive in the teacher a general spirit of child observation. Another application of the scientific attitude is found in the insistence upon the liberty of the child as a prerequisite of the scientific study of educational data. "If a new and scientific pedagogy," says Madam Montessori, "is to arise from the *study of the individual*, such study must occupy itself with the observation of *free* children." Further, the adaptation of Seguin's material to a disciplinary end would seem to have had its origin in the wish on the part of Madam Montessori to utilize her scientific study of sense-experience. It must be said, however, that while Madam Montessori's interest in the scientific attitude is entirely praiseworthy, her actual science cannot be so highly commended. Her biology is not always above reproach, as, for example, the alleged disinfecting influence of garlic upon the intestines and lungs. She generalizes unscientifically as to the condition of contemporary educational thought and practice from observation limited, it would seem, to the Italian schools. If she had known more of what was being thought and done elsewhere, her discussions would have been saved some blemishes and her system some serious omissions. Her psychology in particular would have been improved, had she known better what Wundt was doing in Germany, to mention no other names.

While these shortcomings are mentioned, we should not fail to call attention to an evidence of scientific attitude and faith too seldom found in the teaching world — be it said to our shame. Few in the history of education have been capable of breaking so completely with the surrounding school tradition as has this Italian physician. To set aside tradition for science is no common achievement. That the innovator is a woman will seem to some all the more remarkable. With the true scientific spirit of experimentation Madam Montessori has devised a practice and an institution. Such a consciously scientific creation stands in marked contrast with the conservatism and mystical obscurantism which but too widely characterize kindergarten education in America and elsewhere. Whatever opinion be held as to the success of the effort, no one can fail to approve Madam Montessori's thoroughgoing attempt to found a complete school procedure upon her highest scientific conceptions.

In the discussion which follows it will be assumed that the reader is acquainted with Madam

THE MONTESSORI SYSTEM

Montessori's chief work, *The Montessori Method*,[1]
and also with the didactic apparatus itself. The
effort will be to examine the Montessori system
and to appraise its worth to American education.
Especial attention will be given to the merits of
the Casa dei Bambini as a rival to the kindergarten. Owing to limitations of space, only the
most characteristic elements of the system will
be considered.

[1] Frederick Stokes Company, New York, 1912.

II

EDUCATION AS DEVELOPMENT

THAT education should be considered as a development from within is a principal doctrine with Madam Montessori. The idea, of course, is an old one. Rousseau, Pestalozzi, and Froebel are among its most conspicuous exponents. The value of this point of view in the formation of our present educational practice is undoubted. The limitations of the doctrine, however, have not always been clearly seen. Education as development has been likened to the care given to some rare and unknown plant. The gardener seeks to discover and supply the conditions under which the plant can show its character or nature most completely. But the analogy is clearly deficient, else anger and other ugly or erratic impulses should be expressed as completely and directly as those we prize more highly. The ill odor attaching to the word "whim" illustrates the point and shows the way. Life, indeed, consists in the expression of what we are, but under such conditions that the net result shall, in the long run, bring the fullest expression to all concerned. The conditions under which this proper expression may take place — so far as these have originated with man — make up the content of the cultural environment. Man has learned certain ways of doing things that he might the better express himself. This is as true of clothing, shelter, methods of procuring and preparing food, of art and literature, as it is of ethical concepts and legal procedure. The "funded capital of civilization" consists exactly of all the devices thus far contrived for the fullest expression of what we are, for our fullest possible development.

Education is thus, in truth, the completest possible development of the individual; but the task of securing such a development is as great as is the complex of civilization. Expression involves as truly the mastering of this complex as it does the living-out of the impulsive life. More exactly, the two elements of mastering the environment and expressing one's self are but outer and inner aspects of one and the same process; each either meaningless or impossible apart from the other. Only in this larger sense can it be said that education is the development of the individual.

Some, on the contrary, have taken the position,

previously suggested, that in the child's nature as given at birth there is contained — in some unique sense — all that the child is to become, and this in such fashion that we should tend the child as the gardener does the plant, assured that the natural endowment would properly guide its own process of unfolding. Such is Madam Montessori's view. "The child is a body which grows and a soul which develops; . . . we must neither mar nor stifle the mysterious powers which lie within these two forms of growth, but must *await from them* the manifestations which we know will succeed one another." "The educational conception of this age must be solely that of aiding the psycho-physical development of the individual." "If any educational act is to be efficacious, it will be only that which tends to *help* toward the complete unfolding" of the child's individuality.

Such a doctrine of education has borne good fruit; but there is danger in it. It has led in the past to unwise emphasis and to wrong practice. We have already seen that it carries with it a depreciation of the value rightly belonging to the solutions that man has devised for his ever-recurring problems. In fact, such a theory leads easily, if not inevitably, to Rousseau's opposition

to man's whole institutional life. It further fails
to provide adequately for the most useful of mod-
ern conceptions, that of intelligent, self-directing
adaptation to a novel environment. If development be but the unfolding of what was from the
first enfolded, then the adaptation is made in
advance of the situation, and consequently without reference to its novel aspects. Such a form
of predetermined adaptation proves successful
in the case of certain insects, as the wasp; for
there the environment is relatively fixed. With
man, however, each generation finds — and
makes — a new situation. If education is to pre-
pare for such a changing environment, its fundamental concept must take essential cognizance
of that fact. Still further, this erroneous notion
of education gives to the doctrine of child liberty
a wrong and misleading foundation. If the child
already uniquely contains that which he is properly destined to manifest, then the duty of the
educator is to allow the fullest expression of
what is implicitly given. But such a doctrine of
liberty is notoriously disastrous. The result has,
therefore, been that many have opposed every
scheme of liberty in the schoolroom. By putting
the demand for liberty on a false basis, its friends
have too often proved its worst foes. It would not

be fair to Madam Montessori to say that she herself draws all of these objectionable conclusions from her doctrine of the nature of education. She does not. She has not thought consecutively enough. But the conclusions are there to be drawn. They have been drawn from logically similar doctrines at other times. (We must, therefore, reject Madam Montessori's interpretation of the doctrine of development as inadequate and misleading. The useful elements of this doctrine are covered up in error whenever development is identified with the mere unfolding of latency.

III

THE DOCTRINE OF LIBERTY

THE question here raised is that of the degree to which the child shall by his own choice determine his own activities at school. It was Rousseau who first brought this problem prominently forward. His advocacy of the educational utilization of liberty has profoundly influenced all subsequent thought. Froebel emphasized the same doctrine, but placed it rather on the false basis discussed in the preceding chapter. In contemporary education, Professor Dewey is the most prominent exponent of the general point of view.

In the preceding chapter we saw that some writers, including Madam Montessori, are inclined to limit the concept of development to the mere unfolding of what has from the first been implicitly present. Such writers are further inclined to consider the doctrine of liberty as simply a corollary to this conception of development. That is to say, if the child's whole future life is in fact already uniquely present in his nature at birth, then manifestly, that nature must be allowed to unfold. This is the point of departure for Madam Montessori's doctrine of liberty. "We cannot know," she says, "the consequences of suffocating *a spontaneous action* at the time when the child is just beginning to be active: perhaps we suffocate *life itself*. Humanity shows itself in all its intellectual splendor during this tender age . . . and we must *respect* religiously, reverently, these first indications of individuality. If any educational act is to be efficacious, it will be only that which tends to *help* toward the complete unfolding of this life. To be thus helpful it is necessary rigorously to avoid the arrest of spontaneous movements."

But nearer, apparently, to Madam Montessori's heart is the liberty to be accorded the child as an object of scientific study. "The school must permit the *free, natural manifestations* of the *child* if in the school scientific pedagogy is to be born." The aim is to accord to the child "complete liberty." "This we must do if we are to draw from the observation of his spontaneous manifestations conclusions which shall lead to the establishment of a truly scientific child-study." A further reason for the use of liberty is found in Madam Montessori's belief that "discipline must come through liberty." By discipline she means self-control. "We call an individual disciplined when he is master of himself." To this fruitful suggestion we shall later return.

From these various considerations a system has been devised which accords a remarkable degree of freedom to the individual children of the Montessori schools. A contrast between the Montessori school and the kindergarten of the more formal and traditional type may serve to give a clearer picture of the Montessori procedure, and consequently of the Montessori conception of liberty as it appears in practice. The most evident difference is seen in the function of the teacher. The kindergartner is clearly the center and arbiter of the activity in the room. The Montessori directress seems, on the contrary, to be at one side. The kindergartner contemplates at each moment the whole of her group; the directress is talking usually to one alone — possibly to two or three. The kindergarten children are engaged in some sort of directed group activity; each Montessori child is an isolated worker, though one or more comrades may look on and suggest. The arrangement of the room shows the same contrast. The kindergarten has a circle about which all may gather, and tables for group activity. The Montessori room is fitted, preferably, with individual tables, arranged as the children will. (In the writer's observation, there has been little deviation, however, from arrangement in formal rows.) Montessori provides long periods, say of two or more hours, while the kindergarten period rarely goes beyond a half-hour. During the period assigned for that purpose practically all of the Montessori apparatus is available for any child (except for the very youngest or the newest comers), and the child makes his choice freely. The kindergartner, on the other hand, decides very nicely what specific apparatus shall be used during any one period. The Montessori child abides by his choice as long as he wishes, and changes as often as he likes; he may even do nothing if he prefers. The child in the traditional kindergarten uses the same apparatus throughout the period, and is frequently led or directed by the teacher as to what he shall do. At other times he may be at liberty to build or represent at will whatever may be suggested by the "gift" set for the period. The Montessori child, each at his own chosen task, works, as stated, in relative isolation, his nearest neighbors possibly looking on. The directress, perchance, will not interpose in the slightest throughout a whole period. In the kindergarten all the children at the table, for example, are directed — in the large, at least — by the teacher, and all keep more or less together in what they are doing. The Montessori child learns self-reliance by free choice in relative isolation from the directress. He learns in an individualistic fashion to respect the rights of his neighbors. The kindergarten child learns conformity to social standards mainly through social pressure focused and brought to bear in a kindly spirit by the kindergartner. His self-reliance tends to be the ease of mind resulting from conscious mastery of customs, adult-made and adult-directed. Consciousness of superiority, too, has at times its part in his self-reliance. It is thus clearly evident that in the Montessori school the individual child has unusually free rein.

With so much liberty in the Montessori school it would be easy to suppose that anarchy must ensue. Such has not proved the case. In the first place, the directress is not to allow   useless or dangerous acts, for these must be suppressed, destroyed." "The liberty of the child should have as its *limit* the collective interest." "Absolute rigor" is in extreme cases permitted. While these statements might be so interpreted as to imply coercion and suppression, there is in practice little need of positive restraint, much less than one would have supposed. On a certain visit the writer saw one boy in a sudden temper pull another's hair, but the encounter subsided as quickly as it arose, and no notice was taken of the episode by any one. On the whole, the children worked as busily as ants about a hill. At times the noise would prove a little trying to one brought up in the belief that children should be seen and not heard. Probably, however, any protest against the noise would be rather conventional than just. To the writer the suggestion of great individual liberty proves very attractive.

What is the desirable and feasible thing to do in this matter of liberty in school activities? It will perhaps suffice for our purpose to consider briefly four questions suggested by experience with the kindergarten: (1) Why allow the child to exercise his choice? (2) With free choice granted, how is coöperation in group activity to be secured? (3) How is the child to secure the requisite knowledge and skill? (4) How shall we secure conduct that conforms to social standards? In strictness these questions seem hopelessly to overlap; it is hoped, however, that this difficulty may be avoided in the discussion.

Why allow the child to exercise free choice? It

might be replied that the presumption of liberty lies with the individual; that any infringement must be justified. The writer would be willing to accept this reasoning, even in the case of the child. We need not, however, base our argument on this point of view. Other, and to some more convincing, considerations may be urged. In a democracy, self-direction must be the goal of education. How shall the child become self-directing? Can one learn to swim out of water? To become self-directing one must enter life itself, where decision and choice and responsibility hold sway. This seems undoubted in the realm of conduct as an exercise of "will"; it is equally true of the more intellectualistic aspect of thinking. Under Professor Dewey's influence it has become a commonplace that no thinking worthy the name goes on apart from a felt problem, a thwarted impulse. The problems set by the teacher are too often not so felt by the children. A reported or artificial problem has little gripping effect. The real problem arises when the current of real life is for the time dammed. Under such conditions, the child puts heart and soul into the situation in a genuine effort to straighten things out. It is then, if ever, that there is training of "mind" or "will." But evidently the current of real life — in the sense here used — can flow only when the child has freedom to choose, to express himself. And life does not flow in twenty-minute periods. Let the child get genuinely interested, and the short period proves all too short.[1] If school life is to repeat and make possible actual life, the tyranny and artificiality of the short period and of over-much direction by the teacher must go. Real thinking and real conduct demand freer rein. Postponing for the time the discussion of Madam Montessori's curriculum, it appears that she and our more liberal American kindergartens are here well in advance of Froebel and the traditional kindergarten. The absence of a detailed program and of excessive direction from above afford — in this respect, at least — a fuller opportunity for genuine self-expression.

The discussion so far given prepares for our second question: How shall we secure coöperation if the children be allowed freedom of choice? We now feel like turning the question about: How can coöperation be secured except by the spontaneous impulse of the children themselves?

---

[1] The objection here urged against the short period is based, of course, on an assumed régime of relative freedom. If tasks, however, are to be set, as is common in our schools, the short period may be a psychologic necessity.

THE MONTESSORI SYSTEM

If cooperation be forced from without, is it not largely a sham and a counterfeit? The desirable group work is that joint activity which springs from the felt necessity of joint action. We are here but repeating the discussion of the preceding paragraph. What we wish, then, is to put the children into such socially conditioned environment that they will of themselves spontaneously unite into larger or smaller groups to work out their life-impulses as these exist on the childish plane. From these considerations we criticize both Montessori and Froebel, the one that she does not provide situations for more adequate social coöperation, the other that the coöpera tion comes too largely from outside suggestion and from adult considerations.

If our discussion of freedom has so far led us to emphasize the advantage of free choice, the two remaining of the four questions imply limitations in the exercise of such freedom. It has always been known that following one's own sweet will does not of necessity bring either the most of knowledge or the best of conduct. It is, indeed, the insistent obtrusion of this easily observed fact that has led parents and teachers in all times to set such severe limitations upon the free expression of the child's spontaneous impulses. If we were here concerned with the education of children of all ages, our task would be more difficult. As, however, we are more interested in the kindergarten age, the problem may not prove insoluble.

Before asking how the child shall secure the requisite knowledge and skill, let us ask how much of these he should possess at the end of the sixth year? Is this so great in amount, or so difficult of acquisition, that only formal teaching, enforced by external compulsion, will suffice to give it? A child entering the primary school should — by common consent, at least — not be required to present very specific entrance preparation. It is still true that he should have organized and hold available a general range of experience. We need not ask precise agreement, but in general he should have a certain use of the mother tongue. He should know the names and uses of many common things of ordinary life about him. He should know certain of the commonest physical properties of things. In certain ordinary manual activities it were well for him to have reasonable skill, using scissors, paste, a pencil or crayon, and colors. If he is able to stand in line, march in step, and skip, so much the better. He should know some enjoyable games and songs, and some of the popular stories, suited to his age. He should be able, within reason, to wait on himself in the matter of bathing, dressing, etc. Propriety of conduct of an elementary sort is expected.

Does any one question that knowledge and skill such as this can be gained incidentally in play by any healthy child? Indeed, so satisfied have many parents been of this point that they believe a kindergarten course unnecessary, feeling that home life suffices. Without accepting such a position, we may ask whether a group of normal children playing freely with a few well-chosen toys under the watchful eye of a wise and sympathetic young woman would not only acquire all this knowledge and skill and more, but at the same time be enjoying themselves hugely? Surely, to ask the question is to answer it. In this instance the doctrine of freedom is practically the doctrine of interest. As difficult as the problem of interest for the upper grades seems to be, here in the kindergarten age there is little difficulty apart from our lack of faith to try, or of skill to execute. We can leave a great deal more to the natural working-out of the child's spontaneous interest than many of us have dared to believe. And curiously enough, the kindergartner, in spite of Froebel's faith in childhood, is too often the opponent of real freedom. It is here as much as anywhere else that Madam Montessori, exemplifying Professor Dewey's teaching, will affect the practice of education in America.

There yet remains the fourth question, the relation of free choice to right conduct. That the demands of propriety limit the natural freedom of conduct need not be questioned. The real question is, How can we so condition the child that he shall best be brought to observe the obligations that devolve upon him? In particular, what is the relation of this proposed management to the child's spontaneity? The preceding considerations have disposed us to favor a relatively free expression of the childish nature. Is it different here? Shall we agree with the Director, Signor Stratico of Rome, in opposing the Montessori system "because it makes little anarchists"? Perhaps democratic America had already, before the advent of Madam Montessori, arrived at a more approving attitude.

We may as well admit at the outset that certain of the child's natural impulses, probably acquired by the race under widely differing conditions of survival, cannot now be expressed in the manner and at the time in which they normally present themselves. Such manifestations we must either starve off, for the time suppress, or greatly redirect. Certain other impulses will need less of redirection; still others, only opportunity for expression. Probably in the effort to suppress or redirect impulses a certain amount of positive pain association ("punishment") will prove necessary, particularly during the prekindergarten age; but, on the whole, the most effective plan of managing the recalcitrant impulses will be to encourage and feed those others which are naturally leading in the proper directions. Thus again we find approval for positive self-expression. It is this principle that Madam Montessori has in mind when she speaks of "active discipline." Our fathers expressed the same in more theological guise when, speaking through Dr. Watts, they said, —

"Satan finds some mischief still for idle hands to do."

There is yet another and perhaps more important respect in which the principle of free expression leads to proper habits of conduct. Ethics, propriety of conduct in general, is perhaps best conceived as the proper way of " getting along " with others, of adjusting one's self satisfactorily

— to all concerned — to a social situation. If this be so, we could say almost *a priori* that only by mingling with people under normal conditions can one learn to "get on" with them. The stimuli of social approval and disapproval are, after all, about the strongest spurs for directing conduct aright that we know. Child and adult, alike, yield to the demand of their fellows. What we wish, then, is to put children of the kindergarten age under such conditions of companionship that they will learn gradually the fine art of living with their fellows. To this end adult supervision, true enough, will be necessary. It is just here that the kindergarten finds its chief *raison d'être*. The teacher must at times intervene to draw distinctions and direct wisely the course of approval. The real agency, however, is the child's own comrades.

It is difficult, then, to escape the conclusion, from whatever standpoint we view the situation, that the relatively free expression of the child's natural impulses — safeguarded, as discussed — is the efficient plan for his proper rearing. Such freedom is necessary if the child is to enter with full zest into actual coöperation, and into the acquisition of those habits of knowledge and skill which are properly to be expected. The same freedom is necessary if he is to grow into adequate self-reliance, and, at the same time, into the adequate control of self in the appreciation of the rights of others. From such considerations we highly approve Madam Montessori's reëmphasis of the doctrine of liberty. In the practical outworking of her idea she has set an example to home, to kindergarten, and to primary school. There must be less of doing for the child where he can do for himself; less of the short-period program, where interest is too highly excited only to be too soon dissipated; less of minute direction by mother, kindergartner, or teacher; — in short, more of opportunity for the child to lead a simple, healthy, normal life.

IV

ADEQUACY OF SELF-EXPRESSION IN THE MONTESSORI SYSTEM

FREEDOM apart from self-expression is a contradiction of terms. The discussion of Madam Montessori's doctrine of freedom given in the preceding chapter is, therefore, incomplete without a consideration of the adequacy of self-expression allowed by her system. The didactic apparatus which forms the principal means of activity in the Montessori school affords singularly little variety. Without discussing here the grounds for this restriction, it suffices to say that this apparatus by its very theory presents a limited series of exactly distinct and very precise activities, formal in character and very remote from social interests and connections. So narrow and limited a range of activity cannot go far in satisfying the normal child. It is, of course, true that a child finds pleasurable content in an activity which to the adult would seem hopelessly formal, even to the point of drudgery. The small child who took off the box-top and put it back on for seventy-nine times in succession furnishes a good illustration. In the same way, we must not hastily conclude that no child could enjoy the relatively formal exercises of the didactic apparatus. Mechanical manipulation has strong attractions for childhood. But after all is said, the Montessori school apparatus affords but meager diet for normally active children. Further, while happy childhood knows no stronger or more fruitful impulse than imaginative and constructive play, still, in these schools *playing* with the didactic apparatus is strictly forbidden, and usually no other play-material is furnished. Madam Montessori has, in fact, been publicly quoted as saying, "If I were persuaded that children needed to play, I would provide the proper apparatus; but I am not so persuaded." The best current thought and practice in America would make constructive and imitative play, socially conditioned, the foundation and principal constituent of the program for children of the kindergarten age, but Madam Montessori rejects it. Closely allied with play is the use of games. One finds more attention paid to this, but the games seen in the Montessori schools of Rome are far inferior in every respect to those found in the better American kindergartens. Madam Montessori herself seems, from her use of the very word "game," to have a most narrow and restricted conception of what games are, and of what they can do. Those more advanced forms of self-expression, drawing and modeling, are, on the whole, inferior to what we have in this country. Modeling is, in fact, hardly at all in evidence. Drawing and painting are occasionally good, but frequently amount to nothing but the coloring of conventionalized drawings furnished by the teacher. Stories have little or no place — a most serious oversight. There is very little of dramatization. On the whole, the imagination, whether of constructive play or of the more æsthetic sort, is but little utilized. It is thus a long list of most serious omissions that we have to note.

A partial offset to these deficiencies is found in the "practical life" activities. These undoubtedly offer expression to a side of child nature too often left unsatisfied. To do something that counts in real life, not simply in the play world, is frequently one of the keenest pleasures to a child. It should be remarked, too, that the deficiencies noted are not inherent in the use of the more admirable features of the Montessori system; that is to say, we can borrow the good from this source without giving up the good we already have. Doubtless if Madam Montessori had herself known more of better educational practice elsewhere, she would have incorporated some, perhaps all, of the features the absence of which e here regret.

It is evident from the foregoing that, after all as been said, the Montessori curriculum affords very inadequate expression to a large portion of child nature. Such a limitation of opportunity is, in effect, nothing less than repression, a repression destructive alike of happiness and mental growth. Moreover, since expression is the means to the acquisition of the culture of the race, the deficiency in expression is serious, whether it be looked at from the point of view of the child and his present happiness and growth, or from the point of view of culture and of the child's preparation for participation therein. From every consideration, the proposed curriculum proves inadequate and unduly restrictive.

V

AUTO-EDUCATION

Auto - education as conceived by Madam Montessori is the necessary correlative of a régime of freedom. From directed activity alone can training come, but for her direction must not contravene the child's freedom. With the teacher thus ruled out, and the child's self - direction inadequate, resort is had to the apparatus. In place of the old - time teacher, says Madam Montessori, "we have substituted the didactic material, which contains within itself the control of error, and which makes auto-education possible to each child."[1] Does the reader ask how this is done? Let the cylinder box answer. This is a wooden block, in which are holes of varying depths. To each hole belongs a cylinder which exactly fills it. All the cylinders are removed, and the child proceeds to replace them. "If he mistakes, placing one of the objects in an opening that is too small for it, he takes it away, and proceeds to make trial, seeking the proper opening.

[1] *The Montessori Method*, p. 371.

If he makes a contrary error, letting the cylinder fall into an opening that is a little too large for it, and then collects all the successive cylinders in openings just a little too large, he will find himself at the last with the big cylinder in his hand, while only the smallest opening is empty. The didactic material *controls every error*. The child proceeds to correct himself."

The auto-education is for Madam Montessori the only true education. "This self-correction leads the child to concentrate his attention upon the differences of dimensions, and to compare the various pieces. It is in just this comparison that the psycho-sensory exercise lies." "It is the work of the child, the auto-correction, the auto-education which acts."

It is impossible not to sympathize with Madam Montessori's intention in emphasizing this notion of auto-education. The more fully the child can learn from his own experience without any telling from the teacher, the more fully is his knowledge his own. If he can feel for himself the problem, if he can work out for himself a plan of solution, and if finally he can ascertain by tests of his own that his solution is correct — if these results can be attained from any plan, then surely that plan is a good one.

AUTO-EDUCATION

When, however, we turn from the general conception to the specific working of Madam Montessori's auto - education, we find that what should be the counterpart of generous liberty, amid many and varied opportunities, has in effect shrunk to a relatively mechanical manipulation of very formal apparatus. The didactic apparatus is in intention so devised that with each piece one, and only one, line of activity is feasible. Thus to the properly initiated child the sight of the cylinder box described above suggests only the taking-out of the cylinders and putting them back (any side suggestion, as improvising a wagon, is effectually suppressed). And the box is further so contrived that there is only one order in which the cylinders will fit. "The didactic material," in this case, at least, "controls every error." (It is in this limited fashion that Madam Montessori provides self-education.) It is under such conditions that the directress keeps herself in the background and relies upon the cylinder box to set the problem and test the solution. Surely it is a naïve trust in a very generous transfer of training which can see appreciable profit in so formal and restricted a scheme of auto - education. As applied by Madam Montessori, we must conclude, then, that auto-education is more of a wish than a fact. In her scheme it is too intimately bound up with the manipulation of the didactic apparatus to afford outside thereof the fruitful suggestion of wise procedure.

If, on the other hand, we consider life itself and the situations that arise therefrom, we find abundant instances of evident self-education. A boy trying to drive a nail soon learns whether he is hitting it on the head. A pair of roller skates suggest their own problem with a minimum of explanation; they also test admirably the solution proffered. The sight of possible playmates suggests socially conditioned activity; the same children pass upon the newcomer's ability to participate successfully. We may generalize by saying that self-education is the concomitant of attempted purpose: whenever one can see the connection between effort and success he is on the road to the perfected activity. We are then led again to practically the same conclusion as previously reached elsewhere: The nearer to the conditions of normal life that the school life can be brought, the more will real problems present themselves naturally (and not artificially at the say-so of the teacher). At the same time, the practical situation which sets the problem will test the child's proposed solution. This is life's auto-education and a right good pedagogic scheme it is. If Madam Montessori's term and general discussion can help us attain in practice what we have for years admitted in theory, she will have an honorable part in the reorganization now under way of our kindergarten and early primary education; but the formal auto-education based on the didactic apparatus is at present more of a danger than a help.

VI

EXERCISES OF PRACTICAL LIFE

THE Montessori schools were first devised in connection with an unusually intelligent effort at improving certain tenement houses in Rome. The families being poor, it was an assistance to them for the school to take care of the children during as much of the day as possible. Accordingly, the length of the school day advocated by Madam Montessori extended to eight or ten hours according to season. There was thus a concentration of authority and responsibility in the school, which was the more fortunate, since many of the parents had low standards of living. In this way, the "Children's Houses" pay much attention to cleanliness of person and dress. The children are taught to wash their hands, brush their hair, brush their teeth, rinse their mouths, and otherwise care for their bodily and personal needs. The schoolroom is largely kept in order by the children themselves. Since school is held during practically the whole day, a school lunch is necessary, the serving of which is largely the work of the children.

No feature of the Montessori schools has been more commented upon than the skill and deftness with which the children serve these luncheons. Every one who has been present at one of these luncheons will recall with pleasure the eager yet serious interest exhibited by the children, and the success with which tiny tots did what we usually associate solely with older hands. It seems to the writer that we have here once more an instance of putting the school exercises on the plane of normal child-life. Not a few kindergartners — perhaps most of them — know from their own experience how much pleasure children take in such real life matters. The interest is just what we have a right to expect. But what about the skill? It has been said that "not a mistake is made, not a glass is broken, not a drop of soup is spilled." And many friends of the system have asserted that this success is due to the muscular control gained from the use of the didactic apparatus. To these assertions, two remarks may be made. First, although the children do exceedingly well, they still do make lapses. The writer saw soup spilled and mistakes made in distributing lunch-baskets.

His friend saw a glass and a plate broken. Second, there were no evidences of greater skill or ability than could reasonably be expected from the amount of attention paid by the school to the specific exercise itself. Here, as elsewhere, "practice makes perfect."

The question that concerns us, however, is rather the value of such "practical life" activities to our American schools. The long school day is well worth consideration. Where mothers are so closely confined to duties either at home or on the outside that the children cannot receive proper attention, all-day care of the young children by the kindergarten would be highly desirable. Again, in large cities, where opportunities for open air play are few or difficult of management, all children alike would probably benefit from regularly supervised playground exercises. If, then, the kindergartens for the very poor everywhere, and for practically all classes in the large cities, could have an all-day session with much time spent in the open air, the results would probably be highly beneficial. The administrative difficulties connected with such enlarged functions of the kindergarten, while great, would not prove insuperable, if only the desirability of such changes were admitted.

EXERCISES OF PRACTICAL LIFE

What "practical life" exercises should be included in any particular kindergarten will clearly depend upon the community. If the mothers of the children who attend the kindergarten are too busy, or too careless, to see that the children appear in the morning clean and neatly dressed, evidently, the duty of that kindergarten is different from what it would be if the children came from another class of homes. This is to say nothing more than that the curriculum of any school should be a reflex of the needs of the locality served — a principle well recognized in present-day school theory.

In this connection we give most cordial approval to the Montessori practice of letting the child do for himself as far as this may be feasible. In the homes of the poor, necessity may force the child to attend to his wants. Within limits, no training could be better. Among the wealthier, the over-zealous nurse or the indulgent mother too often strives to anticipate each want and effort of the child. No service could be worse directed. As we have already discussed, the claims of morality and intelligence alike demand that the individual come into first-hand contact with actual situations of thwarted impulse. The personal striving and contriving incident to meeting such situations are most wholesome, both to forming intelligent self-reliance and to furnishing the organized data necessary for meeting other situations. Here again we hope much from the Montessori corroboration of a doctrine long and widely preached, but too often disregarded.

The general idea of including among the school exercises such occupations as are mainly valuable from demands of immediate utility is one that proves attractive. It is well recognized that cooking as a school subject, for example, does not arouse the same serious interest among our pupils that it formerly aroused in the home, when the girl who took it up did so to meet the immediate need in the household. The motivation, as we say, is largely lacking in the artificial situation of the schoolroom. If, now, the school can bring into its service something of the gripping interest that attaches to actual and immediate social demand, we shall have the real effort that counts. It must be admitted, however, that this will not hold of all the "practical life" activities, because some of the most insistent of these have never aroused in young children any great internal motivation even in the best homes: washing the face and hands, for example. In such cases, the social approval or disapproval of the schoolroom may prove distinctly helpful in fixing a habit that might never be learned in inferior home surroundings.

While no one could suppose that a curriculum devised for a particular class in Rome would serve, unmodified, in America, we have no hesitation in concluding that we can find suggestion for thought in the long school day, in the practical effort to adapt the school exercises to the needs of the community, and in the possible increase of motivation by the introduction of activities the demand for which is immediate and actual. The whole conception is but part of the world-wide demand that the school shall function more definitely as a social institution, adapting itself to its own environment and utilizing more fully actual life situations.

VII

SENSE-TRAINING BY MEANS OF THE DIDACTIC APPARATUS

No topic is more fundamental to the Montessori method, as understood by its author and her followers, than is its system of sense-training. This was Madam Montessori's initial approach to the study of education; and throughout, it has determined her general point of view. One fourth of the exposition of the system as found in her book is given to this one topic. The didactic apparatus — the most striking feature of the system to the popular mind — was devised to make possible a proper training of the senses. Evidently a careful consideration of this most fundamental part of the system is necessary to any first-hand appreciation of the Montessori method.

While writers on sense - training have not always been careful to differentiate their several theories, we can easily distinguish three separate lines of thinking in this field. The first is that the sense-organ itself can be improved. That is, by systematic training we can, for example, make the eye, as an optical instrument, see more and better. One would thus look out of the trained eye as through an improved telescope. To this notion the two remaining groups of theorists unite in entering a protest. It is not the organ itself, these say, that is changed; a new brain connection has been set up; nothing more. A certain color means that this peach is ready to eat. The child thereafter looks for that color, and notes it when present. A connection has been made between a color — present but previously unnoticed — and the pleasurable expectation of eating the peach. In the sense that he notices more, the child may be said to see more. The difference, however, is not that the optical image has been changed; but only that certain portions of that image are now differently connected in the child's conscious world.

Which of these theories is true? Consider a typical case. Contrast Fenimore Cooper's Indian with a student of languages. Is there any doubt, we may imagine some one asking, that the Indian has a keener eye, that he can see more, and more distinctly? If the trial of strength be in the forest, certainly; the scholar is hopelessly inferior. But bring the Indian into a library. Place before him a page of Latin and a page of French. The two will appear to him alike, a blur of little marks. One glance, however, tells the scholar that the one is Latin and the other French. Which eye, then, really sees the better? Is it not clear that in this case each one sees according to the experience he has had, according to the connections that have been set up? We may safely accept the judgment of the authorities that the sense-organs of the normal child, after the age of two or three, do not in themselves change by training.

Let us now differentiate the second and third theories. These agree in saying that sense-training is a matter of making brain connections. They differ as to how specialized the effect of such training is. The second of the three theories says that if the child has learned to discriminate a certain group of visual forms, he has trained his power of visual discrimination so that thereafter he can the better discriminate any matter of sight. The third says that there is no general power or faculty of visual discrimination or of anything else, that training along one line will carry over into another line only in the degree that the two lines of activity have common elements. The discussion of this point is too lengthy to enter upon here. It suffices to say that after a great deal of investigation there is substantial agreement on the general statement of the third theory as made above. Although there yet remain differences of opinion as to what constitute common elements, the old notion of the existence of faculties of the mind and their consequent general training is now entirely rejected by competent psychologists. We no longer speak of judgment as a general power that can be trained; nor of discrimination, nor of observation.

What practical difference would it make which theory any one might hold? Pedagogically, the applications of the several theories will be widely divergent. If one hold to either the first or the second theories, he will feel that training of some gymnastic kind is the desideratum. He will say, refine the sense of sight; train the general power of visual discrimination. And so, generally, no matter what specific activity you engage in, it is the training that counts. The sense-qualities of objects which you may happen to learn are of relative insignificance; it is the refinement of sense that we seek. The third theory says, on the contrary, it is what you learn that counts. If it be a matter of sense-training, then learn to make those discriminations of color, form, or other sense-quality, that will enter fruitfully into your subsequent life.

Where now stands Madam Montessori? In general she puts great emphasis upon "the education of the senses." That she accepts either the first or second theory would seem to be justified by such a statement as "we must not confuse the education of the senses with the concrete ideas which may be gathered from our environment by means of the senses." And similarly, when she speaks of blindfolding the child "for the education of the senses in general, such as in the tactile, thermic, baric, and stereognostic exercises." Accordingly, such phrases as "education of the stereognostic sense," "education of the chromatic sense," suffice to show either carelessness in thinking or erroneous theory. Similarly for such statements as "the education of the senses makes men observers," "before he can become a doctor, he must gain a *capacity for discriminating between sense-stimuli*." These statements certainly seem to imply a belief in the validity of the general transfer of training; and the more one studies Madam Montessori's writings, the more convinced does he become that she holds to some such position. Apparently she vacillates between the first and second theories.

SENSE-TRAINING

Perhaps the most unmistakable assertion of her position is the following: "It is exactly in the repetition of the exercises that the education of the senses consist; their aim is not that the child shall *know* colors, forms, and the different qualities of objects, but that he refine his senses through an exercise of attention, of comparison, of judgment. These exercises are true intellectual gymnastics. Such gymnastics, reasonably directed by means of various devices, aid in the formation of the intellect, just as physical exercises fortify the general health and quicken the growth of the body." [1]

Here we have most of the earmarks of the old theory of general discipline: "not that the child shall *know* colors, forms . . . but that he refine his senses"; "intellectual gymnastics"; and the same old analogy of mind and body. After the writer had read Madam Montessori's book and had studied the apparatus, he was anxious to ascertain at first hand, if he could, her opinion on the question of the general transfer of mental training. The interview was difficult, as the interpreter was not versed in psychology; but the writer came away convinced that Madam Montessori had up to that time not so much as heard

[1] *The Montessori Method*, p. 360.

of the controversy on general transfer; and that she still held to the doctrine of formal discipline discarded years previously in both Germany and America.

Important as it is to establish Madam Montessori's intention in devising the didactic apparatus, it is equally important — perhaps more so — to ask what is the actual effect of the apparatus when used by children. If we set aside the various buttoning and fastening apparatus as belonging, at least indirectly, to the "practical life" activities, and certain other pieces of apparatus to be discussed in connection with writing, all that is left calls for some form of sense-discrimination. This apparatus is so devised that discriminations may be made either between widely varying stimuli, as a ten-centimeter cube and a one-centimeter cube, or between those which differ only slightly, as the nine-centimeter cube and the eight-centimeter cube. It is a matter of common as well as of scientific knowledge that practice with a series of graduated stimuli results in finer discriminations made more quickly than was at first possible. This will be true, in all probability, of any normal child who may deal with the Montessori apparatus. He will, for example, learn to discriminate infallibly, perhaps, and almost instantly the several weight blocks. If one please so to term it, he has educated his "baric sense." But does this mean that he will be able to distinguish weights in all the ordinary affairs of life? By no means. It may be that he will never use his specific skill at all. He will surely never use it directly, unless there should chance to come a demand for the discrimination of small weights under conditions quite similar to those under which the skill was acquired. His skill, for example, would not suffice to tell whether any given letter would go for two cents. The formal training with the weight blocks would not prove a sufficient substitute for practice with the weight of letters. Has he, then, gained absolutely nothing that will carry over? The extent to which he has profited is still under dispute. He has certainly added to his concept of weight. But the value of this increment is a comparative one, depending upon what he already had got or would otherwise incidentally get, and on the present need for the concept. In general, it seems true that the really necessary concepts, such as of hardness, of heat, or of weight, etc., come in the normally rich experience of the child-life; and conversely, those that do not so come are not then necessary.

In the same way, the training got with each of the several pieces of the didactic apparatus is genuine, but highly specialized, and along lines for the most part so removed from ordinary life conditions that the probability of its functioning directly as skill is very remote: too remote, except possibly with the colors, for us to desire the particular skill attained. Of what advantage will it be to the child to recognize that this given cylinder fits into the second hole of the doubly varying cylinder box? If one should reply that the advantage lies in bringing the child to make discriminations, we should again be in the midst of the discussion as to the general transfer of training. The specific result is certainly the training in this particular discrimination, and not a general power.

It is true that any experience with color or form or weight helps to make one's concepts of these things; and pleasurable experience along any one of these lines will lead the child to look for further allied experiences. It is further true that growth comes from the organization of such experiences, and that this is the training that we really wish. In these ways exercise with this apparatus may be, indeed, will be, of service; because from it comes opportunity for the conscious consideration of such experiences. The formal and mechanical aspect of the training is, however, practically valueless. Any play in which the consideration of a size-experience, for example, enters, will do just as well as does the broad stair of the didactic apparatus. All must approve Madam Montessori's wish to provide more fruitful sense-experiences. Most children need more activity of this kind. The natural fondness of the young child for manipulation and the like is sufficient proof of the fact. Care, too, is necessary that the opportunities offered be sufficiently varied and sufficiently ordered to bring the desired richness of experience. But these considerations — all important though they be — afford no support for the dogma of general transfer, nor do they call for an apparatus so formal and mechanical in character as the system under review offers.

We must, then, take exactly the opposite view from Madam Montessori as to the nature of sense-training. She says that the "aim is not that the child shall *know* colors, forms, and the different qualities of objects." We say that the aim is exactly that he may know such things, and we don't care about his getting any sense-training outside of this. We conclude, accordingly, that Madam Montessori's doctrine of sense-training is based on an outworn and cast-off psychological theory; that the didactic apparatus devised to carry this theory into effect is in so far worthless; that what little value remains to the apparatus could be better got from the sense-experiences incidental to properly directed play with wisely chosen, but less expensive and more childlike, playthings.

VIII

THE SCHOOL ARTS: READING, WRITING, AND ARITHMETIC

No small interest has attached to the reported ease with which children of the Montessori schools learn to read and write. In the popular mind, this comes in an almost occult manner from that individual development which has resulted from the sense-training of the didactic apparatus. A system in which such tangible results ensue from so tangible a set of apparatus is bound to attract attention. When, moreover, it is reported that the children in these marvelous schools are left entirely free, and, as it were, play themselves into this learning, the acme of educational achievement seems, indeed, at hand.

One acquainted, however, with the history of education is prepared to hear of remarkable successes attending the enthusiasm of a new project. Pestalozzi's visitors gave accounts of his success that seem wonderful even to-day. The monitorial schools were similarly acclaimed as ushering in a new era of ease and rapidity in learning. Basedow's daughter, Emilie, apparently surpassed all in her marvelous acquisition of new languages. Ten weeks at the age of three and a half gave her French, and the next year an equal time gave both a speaking and a reading knowledge of Latin. Enthusiasm and the exceptional case always account for much. If there be a permanent contribution, it must be more tangible. Proper scrutiny must be able to find it.

Madam Montessori teaches the beginnings of reading and writing simultaneously. For easier criticism we shall treat the two separately. When we examine the accounts of the teaching of reading in the Montessori schools we find an intelligent utilization of the phonetic character of the Italian language. In this language, to speak generally, one sign represents one sound, and *vice versa.* The method of teaching, then, is to associate the sounds (but not the names) of the several letters with their forms, beginning with the vowels. The names of the letters are not used during this early period. With a one-to-one correspondence of sounds and symbols, the whole alphabet can be readily taught. It is thus easy to build up with letters any given word, or, conversely, to call any word by recalling the sounds attached to its several letters. If, however, one should try to apply this method in America, the unphonetic character of the English language would present formidable difficulties. Any attempt to meet these difficulties could but result in a plan identical with one or another of the quasi-phonetic methods familiar enough to American primary teachers. It thus turns out that the Montessori method of teaching reading has nothing of novelty in it for America. What it can offer has long been present with us, and a vogue previously won has for a decade been passing away.

When we come to writing, the question is somewhat different. Here a special technique has been worked out. From some observations on an indirect method of teaching a defective to sew, Madam Montessori "saw that the necessary movements of the hand *had been prepared without having the child sew*." From this she concluded, in relation to any complex activity, that "we should really find the way to *teach* the child *how*, before *making him execute the task*." "Preparatory movements could be carried on and reduced to a mechanism, by means of repeated exercises not in the work itself, but in that which prepares for it. Pupils could then come to the real work, able to perform it without ever having directly set their hands to it before."

Following up this idea, the process of writing was analyzed into two essential elements, "the muscular mechanism necessary in holding and managing the instrument of writing" and "the visual-muscular image of the alphabetical signs." Special exercises were devised to give the child simultaneous training in these two elements of writing. The apparatus for the first consists of metal geometrical figures and colored pencils. The child takes a triangle, for example, draws about it, and then with a crayon fills in the figure so made. With practice of this sort he gains control in the use of the pencil. The apparatus for giving the second element consists of sand-paper letters mounted on cards and a box of alphabets cut from paper. These letters of both kinds are in clear script. It is in connection with this second element that the reading is taught. When the association of the sound with the form is being taught, the sand-paper letters are used; and the child is required to trace each letter with his index finger as if writing it. They are encouraged to do this repeatedly even with the eyes shut. The child is thus gaining at the same time both visual and muscular images of the letter and associating these with each other and with the sound. As soon as the child knows some of the vowels and consonants, the box of letters is put before him. The directress selects a simple word, pronounces it so clearly as to analyze it into its constituent sounds, and calls for the corresponding letters. The next exercise is for the child to read a word set before him. This he does by calling in succession the sounds corresponding to the several letters. It is evident how essential is the phonetic alphabet to the success of the plan.

After both the elements of the writing process, carried on thus simultaneously, are well fixed, it is a simple matter to have the child write. Indeed, according to reports, this takes place so suddenly as to warrant the phrase "exploding into writing." It is easy to believe this, because the manipulation of the pencil, the muscular image of the word, and the knowledge of the value of the letters are all present. The second and third of these having already been joined, it only remains to connect the first with these two. This is the more readily done since the gradual perfection of the first and second, even as separate activities, has all the while been bringing them closer together. The result is writing. It only remains to be said that this writing, while very slow, is unusually good. The beauty of the writing, quite as much as the reported ease of acquisition, has brought the system into favorable publicity.

The appraisal of Madam Montessori's contribution in the case of writing is difficult. On the whole, it appears probable that she has in fact made a contribution. Of how much value this can prove to those who use the English language is uncertain. Probably experimentation only can decide. Her plan seems so dependent on some single-letter method of learning to read that many will be unwilling even to try it, feeling that previous experimentation on this point is conclusive. The suggested analysis of the process might, however, prove helpful, even if not used exactly as she proposes. We shall await with interest the results of further discussion and experimentation in this field.

As to arithmetic, there is little to be said. About the only novelty is the use of the so-called long stair. This consists of ten blocks, of lengths varying from one to ten decimeters, being in other dimensions the same. These are divided into decimeters, alternate divisions being painted in like colors. These blocks are used in teaching the various combinations which sum ten. On the whole, the arithmetic work seemed good, but not remarkable; probably not equal to the better work done in this country. In particular there is very slight effort to connect arithmetic with the immediate life of the child. Certainly, in the teaching of this subject, there is for us no fundamental suggestion.

The question of introducing the "three R's" into the kindergarten period demands separate consideration, although it is in part bound up with the question of the difficulty of teaching them. In this country we seem pretty well agreed that these subjects had, as a rule, better not be taught prior to the age of six. There is, however, no definite experimental basis for such a judgment; and from this point of view it may well be claimed that the question is as yet an open one. Education, however, is much more than the acquisition of knowledge from books. And there is reason to fear that the presence of books makes more difficult that other part of education. If there be any truth in this point of view, it would seem to hold particularly of the earlier stages of education. From this standpoint some would feel that reading and writing might better be postponed to a later period than put forward to an earlier one. This would not mean that to learn to read and write is in itself very difficult for a child of six; often the reverse is true; but that the presence of these tends to divert the attention of parent, teacher, and child from other and, for the time, possibly more valuable parts of education. Education is life; it must presume first-hand contact with real vital situations. The danger in the early use of books is that they lead so easily to the monopoly of set tasks foreign to child nature, lead so almost inevitably to artificial situations devoid alike of interest and vital contact. An unthinking public mistakes the sign for the reality, and demands formulation where it should ask experience, demands the book where it should ask life. The writer agrees, therefore, with those who would still exclude these formal school arts from the kindergarten period. To him a school for the young without books is Froebel's chiefest glory.

IX

CONCLUSIONS

WE have passed in review the principal features of the Montessori theory and practice. Good points and bad have appeared. Before attempting a summation of the several valuations made, it may be well to ask, Where among other systems of education does this one belong? What is the relation of Madam Montessori to the world's educational thinkers?

When the surmise was made in the first chapter that Pestalozzi formed the background of Madam Montessori's educational philosophy, one might better have said that it was the Rousseau-Pestalozzi-Froebel group which formed that background, although there are more distinct marks of Pestalozzianism than of the others. This group of educational thinkers are differentiated from others by the presence of several characteristics which we find also in the Montessori theory. The revolutionary attitude, the feeling that one is breaking with customary practice, while certainly present, need hardly be mentioned, as this is an element found to a greater or less degree in all reformers. More to the point are: (1) a belief that the child nature is essentially good; (2) that the educational process is fundamentally an unfolding of what was given at birth; (3) a consequent belief in liberty as the necessary condition of this development; (4) the utilization of sense-experiences as means to bringing about the development; (5) a tendency to accept the faculty psychology; (6) the consequent tendency to emphasize the disciplinary aspect of sense-training; and finally (7) the emphasis upon nomenclature in connection with sense-experiences. While not all of these are found with distinctness in the writings of each one of the group, they either are so present or have been drawn as corollaries by followers. They are likewise present in the Montessori theory. When we consider that each of these characteristic doctrines, while containing a greater or less amount of truth, still has needed to be strictly revised in order to square with present conceptions; when we further consider that Madam Montessori's own conception of these doctrines has needed an almost identical revision; when we still further consider that Madam Montessori has confessedly been most influenced by Seguin, whose ideas were first published in 1846; when we consider, in particular, that Madam Montessori still holds to the discarded doctrine of formal or general discipline, — in the light of all these, we feel compelled to say that in the content of her doctrine, she belongs essentially to the mid-nineteenth century, some fifty years behind the present development of educational theory.

If we compare the work of Madam Montessori with that of such a writer and thinker as Professor Dewey, we are able to get an estimate of her worth from still a different point of view. The two have many things in common. Both have organized experimental schools; both have emphasized the freedom, self-activity, and self-education of the child; both have made large use of "practical life" activities. In a word, the two are coöperative tendencies in opposing intrenched traditionalism. There are, however, wide differences. For the earliest education, Madam Montessori provides a set of mechanically simple devices. These in large measure do the teaching. A simple procedure embodied in definite, tangible apparatus is a powerful incentive to popular interest. Professor Dewey could not secure the education which he sought in so simple a fashion.

THE MONTESSORI SYSTEM

Madam Montessori was able to do so only because she had a much narrower conception of
education, and because she could hold to an
untenable theory as to the value of formal and
systematic sense-training. Madam Montessori
centered much of her effort upon devising more
satisfactory methods of teaching reading and
writing, utilizing thereto in masterly fashion the
phonetic character of the Italian language.
Professor Dewey, while recognizing the duty of
the school to teach these arts, feels that early
emphasis should rather be placed upon activities
more vital to child-life which should at the same
time lead toward the mastery of our complex
social environment. Madam Montessori, in a
measure following Pestalozzi, constantly uses
logically simple units as if they were also the
units of psychological experience. In reading and
writing, it is the letter and the single sound, not
the word or thought connection, that receive
attention. Sense-qualities are taught preferably in isolation, apart from life situations. She
speaks also of leading the child "from sensations
to ideas . . . and to the association of ideas."
Professor Dewey insists that the experience is the
unit, and that the logically simple units emerge
for consciousness by differentiation from the

experience. Things, as a rule, are best taught, then, in connection with what is for the child a real experience, when they enter as significant parts into such an experience; and this because learning is essentially the differentiation and organization of meanings. It is, of course, to be borne in mind that a child experience is vastly different from the adult experience. What to a child is a whole satisfying experience, to us may be very fragmentary and disconnected.

But there are even more comprehensive contrasts. Madam Montessori hoped to remake pedagogy; but her idea of pedagogy is much narrower than is Professor Dewey's idea of education. His conception of the nature of the thinking process, together with his doctrines of interest and of education as life, — not simply a preparation for life, — include all that is valid in Madam Montessori's doctrines of liberty and sense-training, afford the criteria for correcting her errors, and besides, go vastly farther in the construction of educational method. In addition to this, he attacked the equally fundamental problem of the nature of the curriculum, saw it as the ideal reconstruction of the race achievement, and made substantial progress toward a methodology of its appropriation. This great problem of the curriculum, it can almost be said, Madam Montessori has, so far, not even seen. While this is no adequate recital of Professor Dewey's contributions, it suffices, in connection with what has been previously said, to show that they are ill advised who put Madam Montessori among the significant contributors to educational theory. Stimulating she is; a contributor to our theory, hardly, if at all.

Is this, then, the final judgment of Madam Montessori's contribution? The question of a permanent contribution turns on whether there have been presented original points of view capable of guiding fruitfully educational procedure. What novel and original ideas have we found that could at the same time bear the scrutiny of criticism? The scientific conception of education is certainly valid. Madam Montessori may, in a way, have come upon it herself; but no one could say that the world did not have a fuller conception of it prior to her. The most that can be claimed on this point is that her advocacy and example have proved stimulating. Her doctrine of education as unfolding is neither novel nor correct. In the doctrine of liberty she has made no theoretical contribution; though probably her practice will prove distinctly valuable. Our

CONCLUSIONS

kindergartens and primary schools must take account of her achievement in this respect. Her doctrine of auto-education will at most provoke thought; the term is good, the idea old. Her utilization of "practical life" activities, more specifically her solution of early tenement-house education, must prove distinctly suggestive. It may well turn out that the Casa dei Bambini is after all her greatest contribution. The sense-training which to her seems most worth while, we decline to accept except in a very modified degree. The didactic apparatus we reject in like degree. Her preparation for the school arts should prove very helpful in Italy. It is possible that her technique of writing will prove useful everywhere. If so, that is a contribution. With this the list closes. We owe no large point of view to Madam Montessori. Distinguishing contribution from service, she is most a contributor in making the Casa dei Bambini. Her greatest service lies probably in the emphasis on the scientific conception of education, and in the practical utilization of liberty.

OUTLINE

I. INTRODUCTION

II. EDUCATION AS DEVELOPMENT

III. THE DOCTRINE OF LIBERTY

OUTLINE

IV. ADEQUACY OF SELF-EXPRESSION IN THE MONTESSORI SYSTEM

VII. SENSE-TRAINING BY MEANS OF THE DIDACTIC APPARATUS

VIII. THE SCHOOL ARTS: READING, WRITING, AND ARITHMETIC

IX. CONCLUSIONS